I0782206

THE MYSTERY OF SMOKEY JOE

by

KAREN NORDSTROM DUGAN

ILLUSTRATED BY MARY GRACE CORPUS

IndieOwlPressKids

4700 Millenia Blvd
Ste 175 #90776
Orlando, FL 32839

info@indieowlpress.com
IndieOwlPress.com

THE MYSTERY OF SMOKEY JOE

Illustrated by Mary Grace Corpus
www.MaryGraceCorpus.com

Edited by Vanessa Anderson at NightOwlFreelance.com

Cover design & Interior layout/design by Vanessa Anderson
Cover art © Mary Grace Corpus

Paperback ISBN: 978-1-949193-99-2
Hardcover ISBN: 978-1-949193-23-7

Printed in the U.S.A.

For my grandchildren

Thomas, Abby, Shellie, and Ethan

"The purity of a person's heart can quickly be measured

by how they regard animals."

– *Théophile Gautier*

THE MYSTERY OF SMOKEY JOE

Along the tree-lined road,
where sumac meets poplar
and oaks are dropping acorns,
a mystery has been brewing.

Unaware they're being watched,
neighbors stroll past and say their casual
hellos to one another as they routinely
walk their dogs.

There have been some changes to this
landscape throughout the years,
but nothing seems to alter
their sleepy routines.

Footstep after footstep, he waits and watches

from his ivy and clover covered fortress.

Here I am, he thinks to himself,

with a long stretch and a wide yawn.

I'm always watching.

Every day he witnesses
dedication and kindness
for the ones they love.

There's one whose frailty
receives constant attention
as they follow behind,
and another who rides in a baby stroller.
He pondered, there's always *something* new
to witness along this road.

Day after day he stays hidden, watching,

until something new catches his eye.

Today happens to be one of those days...

Slowly rising from his safety net,

he creeps forward for a better look.

Not wanting to reveal his location,

he creeps closer.

"This is how a true hobo does it,"

he snickers to himself.

Suddenly, something wafts by his nostrils.

It's a heavenly scent,

not at all like the ones he's used to.

Those smell of creek water and straw,

with a little sewer smell thrown in.

But a hobo will eat anything if they're hungry enough.

Closer and closer to that heavenly scent he creeps,

until finally finding its origin.

Side by side, are two familiar hobos,
eating confidently
with no notice of his presence.

Watching from a safe distance,
he thinks, *now there's a feast!*

Watching and waiting

are the true traits of a hobo's life.

Rarely revealing themselves from their protective cover,

they prefer to remain hidden,

especially until it's quiet and safe.

Eventually, the two hobos seem to have gotten their fill

and stroll off together.

It will be dark soon, he thinks,

and then I'll make my move.

There must be some morsel left for me to savor—

as long as the coast is clear.

After what turns into a longer wait than expected,
he creeps forward toward his prize.
The full moon illuminates his path, making him nervous.
Hobos hate being caught in the light.

But the savory prize that awaits him
will certainly be worth it.
Getting closer to the feast,
he stops and glances side to side.
Yep, no one around, he thinks,
just a little closer now...

Suddenly, a blinding light pierces his eyes.

Drats...everyone knows a hobo's eyes glow in the dark!

He shudders. *Why, it's that lady I've seen before,*

and there's no escape!

Slowly, her gaze falls on him.

He's frozen in dread.

She stands still, speaking with a sweet tone in her voice—

a tone he quickly associates with those footsteps—

the ones that pass by his fortress every day.

They belong to the loving people

who kindly care for their family members.

He'd always wondered what it would be like if

someone like that were to care for him.

13

The lady quietly returns to her fortress,

only to appear again with a new dish and a bowl.

Still frozen with dread, but more curious,

his gaze remains fixated on the lady and the bowl.

"Come here, little one—are you hungry?" she says.

Looking around, he lowers his head,

wondering if she is speaking to him.

Hobos have their own language, so he can't be sure.

Then she places the dish and bowl on the ground

and vanishes.

The blinding light vanishes as well. Not sure if it's a trick

or a trap, he waits.

Then waits some more.

Eventually, he feels confident that he's truly alone
and strolls to see what had been placed on the ground.
After a quick inspection, he begins to taste the source of
the same heavenly scent that had gotten him this far
in the first place.

Quickly looking right then left, down goes his prize.
No straw taste, no creek or sewer smell.
This is a meal fit for a king!

Lapping up the last of his feast,
he quietly patters back to his life of
mystery within his protective hideaway
to continue his hobo routine of
watch and wait.

The dark night passes as quickly as the meal he'd devoured.

The evening sounds and scents are the same as

he nestles deeper into his clover fortress.

The night moves along with the same rhythm he is used to,

but something has shifted in his awareness.

What is it? He thinks deeply to himself.

Something continues gnawing inside him

that begins to disturb his sleep.

There are no unfamiliar noises,

no scents that would alarm a seasoned hobo

such as himself. *What could it be?*

Slowly, like the clacking of the slow-moving train in the

distance, it dawns on him: for the first time in his life,

he is experiencing something called *contentment.*

Certainly, a few kind words and one good meal shouldn't cause my mind to wander this much, he ponders.

But perhaps his street-wise philosophy has been flawed.

Perhaps, he's been seeing things from the only perspective he'd ever experienced.

Was there another perspective?

Yawning wide, he decides to investigate this feeling further, but not before morning.

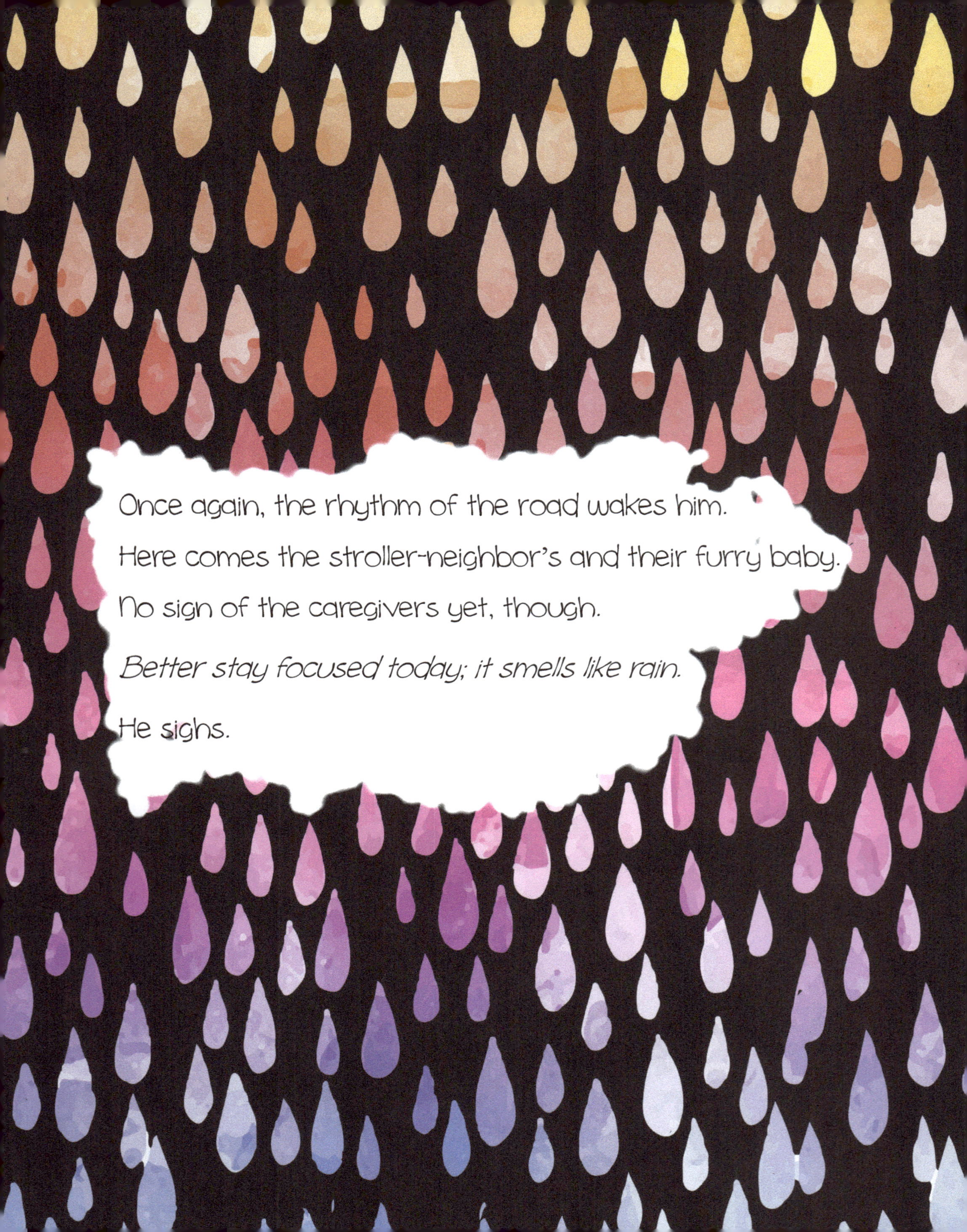

Once again, the rhythm of the road wakes him.

Here comes the stroller-neighbor's and their furry baby.

No sign of the caregivers yet, though.

Better stay focused today; it smells like rain.

He sighs.

As the morning wears on,

his mind keeps returning to the lights that

had caught him by surprise,

and the soothing voice that seemed so welcoming and

kind the night before.

He ponders the possibility that even a street-wise hobo

could use a hand-up from time to time,

but that didn't explain the contentment he'd felt.

Contentment was a new experience.

His daily routine of watching and waiting

suddenly felt boring and unnecessary.

How could this be happening to a

tried-and-true life-long hobo?

He tries to resist the temptation,

but by afternoon he is out of his usual routine

and creeping toward the ivory house...

and the lady with the soothing voice.

Along the road, the poplars are spitting their

leaves—a warning of the colder weather he will

soon have to contend with.

He nestles down to watch.

Sure enough, by early evening, there she is again—

feeding the other two hobos

and waiting for them to finish their meal.

She strolls across her lawn at dusk,

pinching flowers and talking to her resident hobos.

They seem to like it and don't run away.

They follow her, or so it seems.

Then, with the most accurate of moves, she quietly parts

the shrub he thought he had hidden himself so well within,

and says, "Hello again, Smokey Joe—are you hungry, too?"

Startled and frozen where he's crouched, he blinks.

Smokey Joe? Who is that? He jolts back. *Is there someone*

else here?

She quietly stands up and makes her way back to the

porch, then vanishes inside.

Now there comes a time in every hobo's life

where serious decisions must be made.

Looking back up the road toward

his ivy and clover-covered fortress,

he ponders the consequences of leaving it behind.

It would seem that life on the road

certainly has its advantages.

Any self-sufficient hobo would agree.

But all of his survival skills are rivaled

by this newfound sense of contentment.

Does he want to hunker down in his green fortress

day after day, just watching the love these two-legged

caregivers provide for their furry children,

or learn for himself what that's all about?

He swallows hard, and creeps closer

than he ever had before to the ivory fortress.

As the lady appears carrying another plate and bowl,

she is smiling knowingly at him.

Setting down those wonderful morsels once again,

she does something a hobo never experiences:

she reaches out her hand, ever so gently,

and strokes his head as he begins to eat.

Suddenly, he remembers why he couldn't sleep the night before.

23

A memory stirs in the back of his mind.

A memory buried so deep

he fears he might have lost it forever

had she not brought it rushing back with her gentle touch.

The memory of contentment

once again swirls through his body.

Why, I'm not a hobo at all, he realizes.

I'm covered in warm, grey fur

with white whiskers and white paws, he muses.

Hobos don't have those!

As the lady continues to stroke his head,

he continues to eat his wonderful meal,

but much more slowly than the night before.

Sounds are coming from his throat, and the rhythm

is as pleasing as the wonderful morsels before him.

I'm not a hobo, I'm not a hobo,

he realizes happily as he eats.

25

As time passed down the tree-lined street,
his routine changed.

Now he shares contentment with the two others
he once thought were hobos as well.

He has learned the value of kindness and compassion
and prefers it over the isolation of his previous life.

His fortress is still there,
but thick weeds have taken over
where he used to watch and wait.

He now sleeps on a warm blanket under a window,

and his new fortress is filled with the joy

that first brought him the feeling of contentment.

As for the tree-lined road,

the mystery was solved long ago…

There's no longer a hidden neighborhood hobo,

just a contented and furry companion

they all call Smokey Joe.

SMOKEY JOE

Author's Note

6.5 million companion animals enter animal shelters each year. Many lost or abandoned animals find humans whose hearts are open to helping them, but many more arn't that lucky. Imagine a pet who in one moment is safe, warm, and loved by the people they trust and in the next left to fend for themselves. Such was the case with Smokey Joe.

Children can help by donating the cost of a birthday to a local shelter or starting fundraisers in their neighborhoods.

Foster, adopt, donate, or volunteer at your local animal shelters; your heart will thank you for it.

A portion of all book sales will be donated to:

www.aspca.org

www.abandonedpetproject.org

Further Reading

Smokey Joe Goes to the Vet

Forthcoming

Smokey Joe Goes to Heaven

Acknowledgements

Thank you to my husband, Bernie, for your continued love and support for my many interests and the help you provide with "just one more animal" who's been plucked off the road or shows up at our door. Your patience is astounding.

I would also like to thank Mary Hughes for her initial proofreading skills, her gentle encouragement, and kindness as a neighbor and friend.

Thanks to New Cumberland "Write On" writers group members for your critiquing skill and support.

Thank you, Linda Walker, for your guidance, and Stephen Kozan for steering me to the wise and wonderful editor in charge, Vanessa Gonzales, at Night Owl Freelance. Vanessa, you ROCK at helping the beginning writer bring their work to fruition. You glide them along with your wit and wisdom. I can't thank you enough as I look forward to our next collaborative project.

Thank you, Mary Grace Corpus, for your wonderful illustrations and energy. You are an astute illustrator with a multitude of talent at bringing *The Mystery of Smokey Joe* to life!

About the Author

Karen Nordstrom Dugan has studied animal communication, and she works tirelessly rescuing and finding homes for abandoned and unwanted animals. She enjoys history, writing, travel, and is currently writing about her 82nd-Airborne Uncle and the recovery of soldiers missing in action from WWII. She has five adult children, and four grandchildren. She lives near Harrisburg, Pa with her husband, Bernie, and several spoiled fur babies.

www.ingramcontent.com/pod-product-compliance
Lightning Source LLC
Chambersburg PA
CBHW041159300726
48981CB00004B/298